Po...
Po...

B...
Blackcurrant

D0501798

Alice Apple

Peter
Potato

Grace Grape

Wee Willie
Water Melon

The Garden Gang
Stories and pictures by
Jayne Fisher

Other Garden Gang stories

Series 793

Oliver Onion

Ladybird Books Loughborough

It was a sunny morning,
and Oliver Onion got out
of his little bed.
He put on his hat
and brightly polished
shoes.

5

Oliver Onion had only
one boiled egg
and a glass of
fresh orange juice
for his breakfast.
Afterwards he went
to the shop to get
some icecream.
Because it was very hot,
he stripped off his jacket.

"Please may I have
a block of . . .?"
Then he stopped
and looked around
at everyone.
"Why are you all crying?"
he asked.
"Oh I'm so sorry,"
said the shopkeeper,
"but what would you like?"

Well, both you and I know
why they were crying, don't we?
Of course, I'm sure
you know that onions
make you cry, even
if you are happy!
Well, Oliver Onion
knew why they were
crying too.

11

Very slowly he walked
out of the shop,
feeling terribly ashamed
of himself.

When Oliver Onion got home
he went to bed.
In the morning,
he took out the huge,
enormous tin of deodorant
he had bought
and sprayed some
all over himself.

He then went to the shop
and bought everything
he needed, and nobody cried.

He came home
feeling very pleased,
had tea and went to bed.

So if you ever peel,
or see anyone else
peeling onions,
remind them,
and remember yourself . . .

They make you cry!

Tim Tomato

Tim Tomato was
the jolliest person anyone
could ever wish to meet.
He was always smiling
or laughing, and nobody
could stay miserable for long
when he was around.

Now, our story starts
with something being wrong
in the greenhouse.
Everybody was miserable
and nobody ever laughed.
Mark Marrow peered sadly
through the glass
and wondered
why his friends
were so unhappy.
"If only I could
cheer them up,"
he thought.

He tried pulling funny faces
to make them laugh,
and telling funny stories.
But nothing seemed to work;
they looked more
and more miserable.
"The trouble with them,"
he said, "is that they
are all bored.
They need something new
to amuse them."

33

That afternoon
around tea time,
Mr Rake the gardener
came down to the
greenhouse, carrying a
large brown paper bag.
He began to dig a
hole in the soil
and all the
Greenhouse people
looked on, inquisitively.
Mr Rake took out
a young, healthy plant
and put it carefully
into the hole.
Then he watered it and left.

As nothing else happened,
the Greenhouse people
soon lost interest
and went back
to looking miserable.
Later when they
went to sleep
they had forgotten
all about the new arrival.

At once the Greenhouse
people became curious
and began to talk
amongst themselves,
wondering whatever
he was doing.
They waited
with long faces
but all the same, they were
beginning to feel
a little excited.

43

As Tim finished
his sketch he began
to smile to himself.
"What's so funny?"
asked Colin Cucumber, rudely.
"You're not sitting
where I am,"
said Tim Tomato,
and he turned
his sketch pad around
for them all to see.

45

First, when they
saw his drawings,
they were all
quite shocked.
There, before them,
were sketches of
the Greenhouse people
with long, miserable faces.
Colin Cucumber was first
to see the joke
and a smile crept
over other faces,
and the smiles turned
to giggles and laughter.

The next minute,
the greenhouse
exploded with laughter.
The Greenhouse people
rocked about and
held their sides.
Mark Marrow
looked on happily.
"What a clever person
Tim Tomato is,"
he said, and as
he watched them all
he thought that
now the greenhouse
was . . .

49

A very happy place to live!

Paul Pumpkin

Bertie Brussels Sprout

Mark Marrow

Gertrude Gooseberry

Tim Tomato

Patrick Pear

Avril Apricot